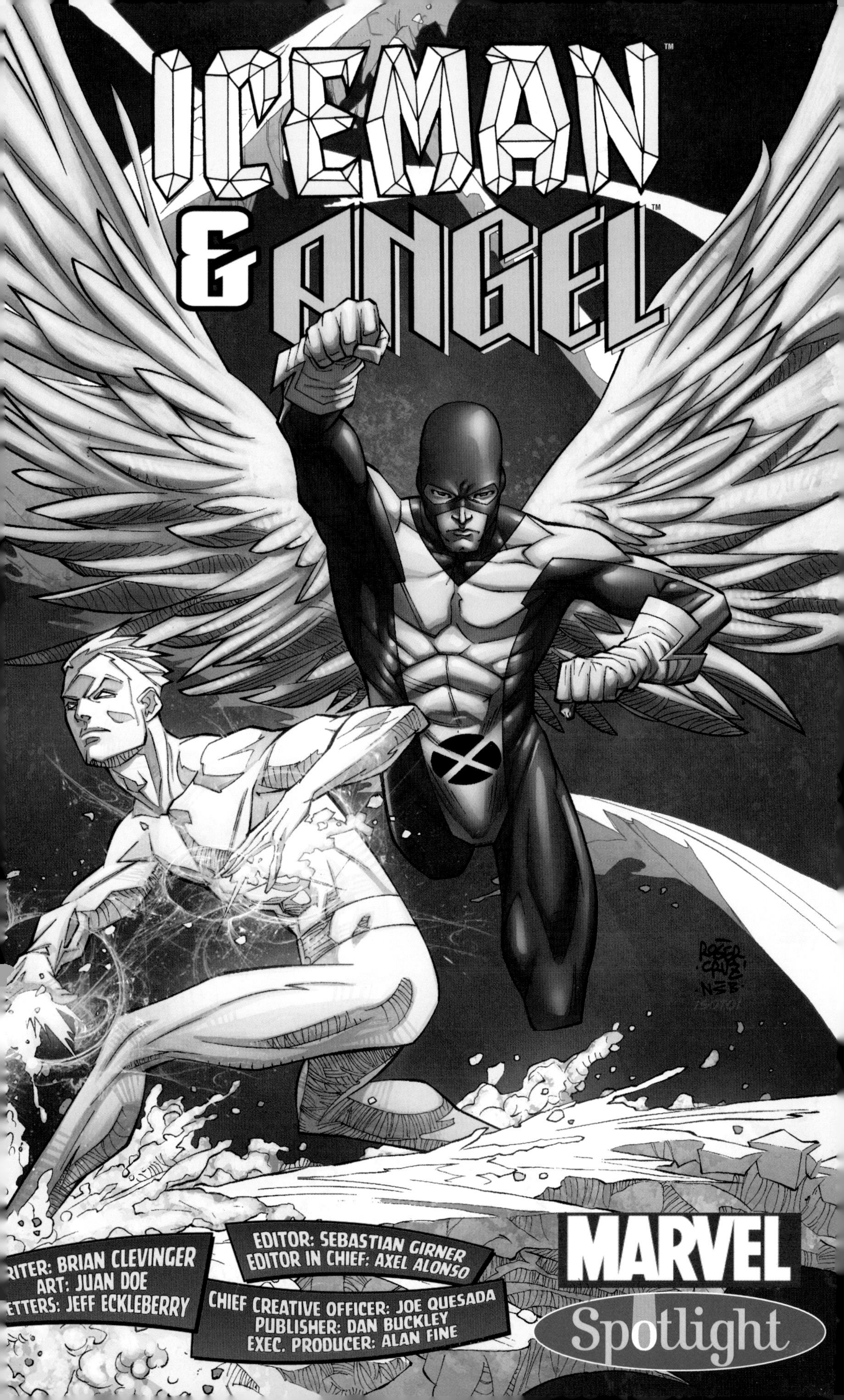
ICEMAN™
& ANGEL™
RITER: BRIAN CLEVINGER
ART: JUAN DOE
ETTERS: JEFF ECKLEBERRY
EDITOR: SEBASTIAN GIRNER
EDITOR IN CHIEF: AXEL ALONSO
CHIEF CREATIVE OFFICER: JOE QUESADA
PUBLISHER: DAN BUCKLEY
EXEC. PRODUCER: ALAN FINE
MARVEL
Spotlight

visit us at www.abdopublishing.com

Reinforced library bound edition published in 2012 by Spotlight, a division of the ABDO Group, 8000 West 78th Street, Edina, Minnesota 55439. Spotlight produces high-quality reinforced library bound editions for schools and libraries. Published by agreement with Marvel Entertainment, LLC. The stories, characters, and incidents mentioned are entirely fictional. All rights reserved. Used under authorization.

Printed in the United States of America, Melrose Park, Illinois.
052011
092011
This book contains at least 10% recycled materials.

Library of Congress Cataloging-in-Publication Data

Clevinger, Brian, 1978-
  Iceman and angel / writer, Brian Clevinger ;art, Juan Doe. -- Reinforced library bound ed.
     p. cm. -- (X-men: first class)
  ISBN 978-1-59961-948-4
  1. Graphic novels. I. Doe, Juan. II. Title.
  PN6728.X2C63 2011
  741.5'973--dc22
                                        2011013930

All Spotlight books are reinforced library bindings
and manufactured in the United States of America.

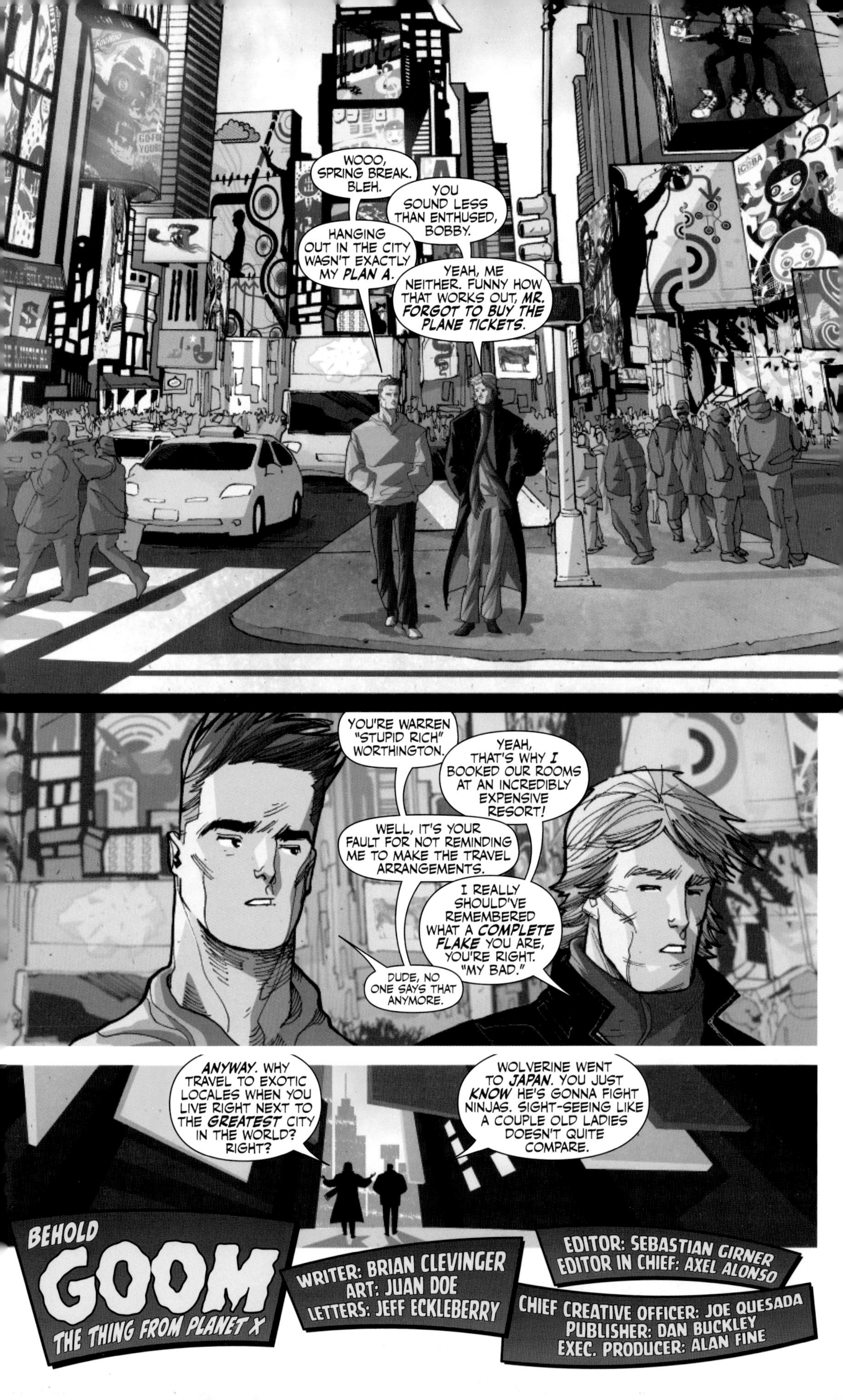
WOOO, SPRING BREAK. BLEH.
YOU SOUND LESS THAN ENTHUSED, BOBBY.
HANGING OUT IN THE CITY WASN'T EXACTLY MY PLAN A.
YEAH, ME NEITHER. FUNNY HOW THAT WORKS OUT, MR. FORGOT TO BUY THE PLANE TICKETS.
YOU'RE WARREN "STUPID RICH" WORTHINGTON.
YEAH, THAT'S WHY I BOOKED OUR ROOMS AT AN INCREDIBLY EXPENSIVE RESORT!
WELL, IT'S YOUR FAULT FOR NOT REMINDING ME TO MAKE THE TRAVEL ARRANGEMENTS.
I REALLY SHOULD'VE REMEMBERED WHAT A COMPLETE FLAKE YOU ARE, YOU'RE RIGHT. "MY BAD."
DUDE, NO ONE SAYS THAT ANYMORE.
ANYWAY. WHY TRAVEL TO EXOTIC LOCALES WHEN YOU LIVE RIGHT NEXT TO THE GREATEST CITY IN THE WORLD? RIGHT?
WOLVERINE WENT TO JAPAN. YOU JUST KNOW HE'S GONNA FIGHT NINJAS. SIGHT-SEEING LIKE A COUPLE OLD LADIES DOESN'T QUITE COMPARE.
BEHOLD GOOM THE THING FROM PLANET X
WRITER: BRIAN CLEVINGER
ART: JUAN DOE
LETTERS: JEFF ECKLEBERRY
EDITOR: SEBASTIAN GIRNER
EDITOR IN CHIEF: AXEL ALONSO
CHIEF CREATIVE OFFICER: JOE QUESADA
PUBLISHER: DAN BUCKLEY
EXEC. PRODUCER: ALAN FINE

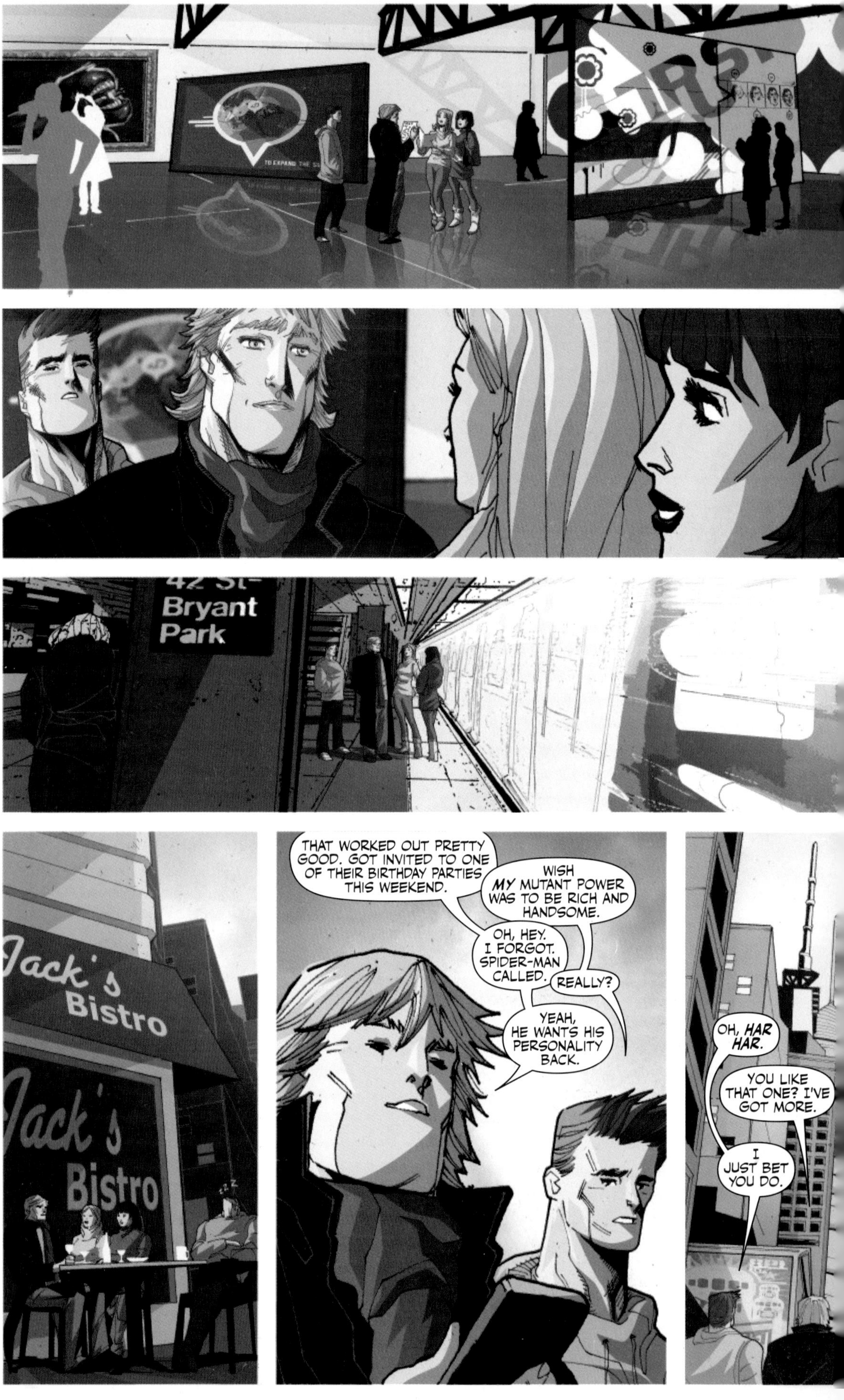

42 St-
Bryant
Park
Jack's
Bistro
Jack's
Bistro
THAT WORKED OUT PRETTY GOOD. GOT INVITED TO ONE OF THEIR BIRTHDAY PARTIES THIS WEEKEND.
WISH *MY* MUTANT POWER WAS TO BE RICH AND HANDSOME.
OH, HEY. I FORGOT. SPIDER-MAN CALLED.
REALLY?
YEAH, HE WANTS HIS PERSONALITY BACK.
OH, *HAR HAR.*
YOU LIKE THAT ONE? I'VE GOT MORE.
I JUST BET YOU DO.

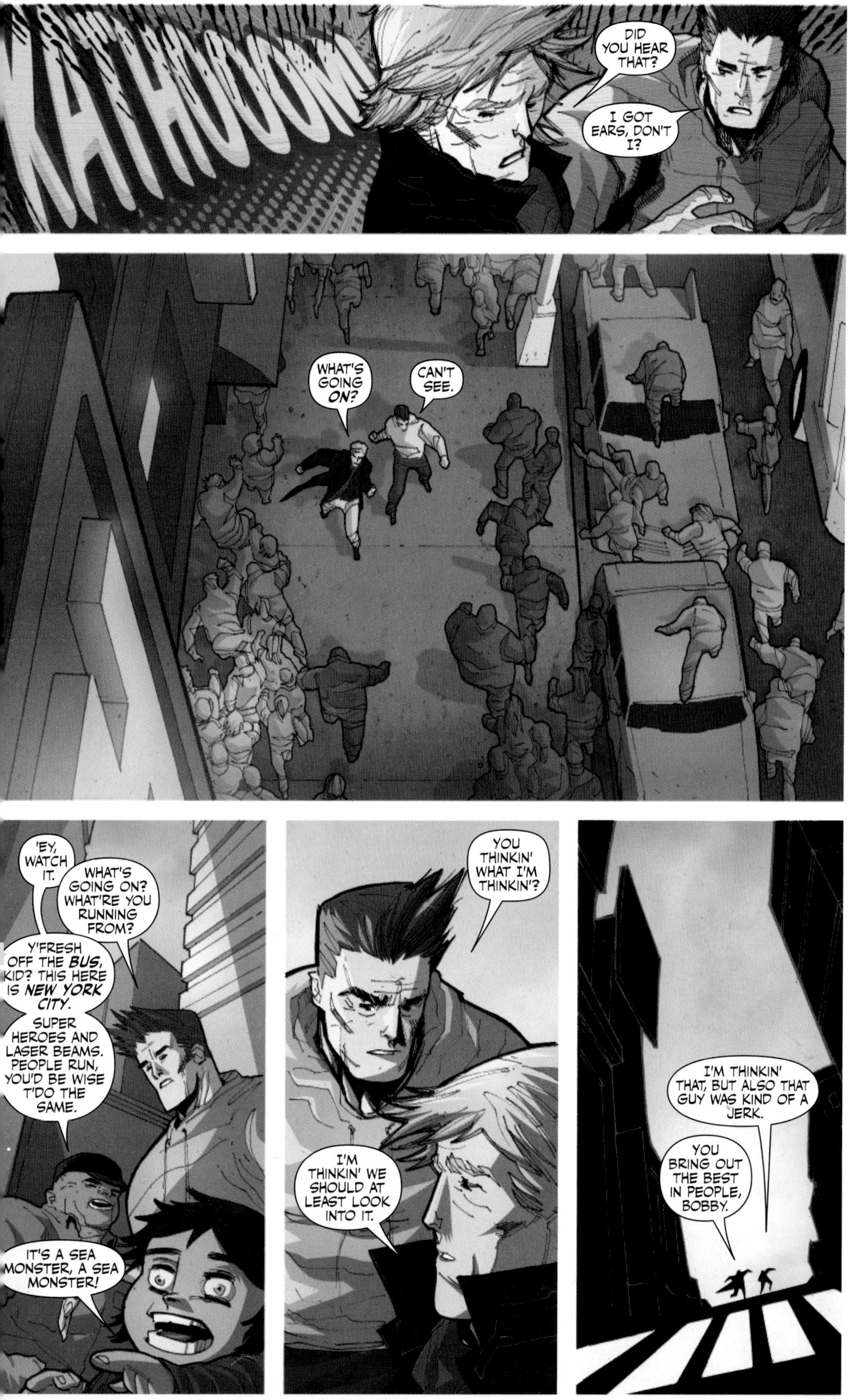
KATHOOOOM
DID YOU HEAR THAT?
I GOT EARS, DON'T I?
WHAT'S GOING ON?
CAN'T SEE.
'EY, WATCH IT.
WHAT'S GOING ON? WHAT'RE YOU RUNNING FROM?
Y'FRESH OFF THE BUS, KID? THIS HERE IS NEW YORK CITY.
SUPER HEROES AND LASER BEAMS. PEOPLE RUN, YOU'D BE WISE T'DO THE SAME.
IT'S A SEA MONSTER, A SEA MONSTER!
YOU THINKIN' WHAT I'M THINKIN'?
I'M THINKIN' WE SHOULD AT LEAST LOOK INTO IT.
I'M THINKIN' THAT, BUT ALSO THAT GUY WAS KIND OF A JERK.
YOU BRING OUT THE BEST IN PEOPLE, BOBBY.

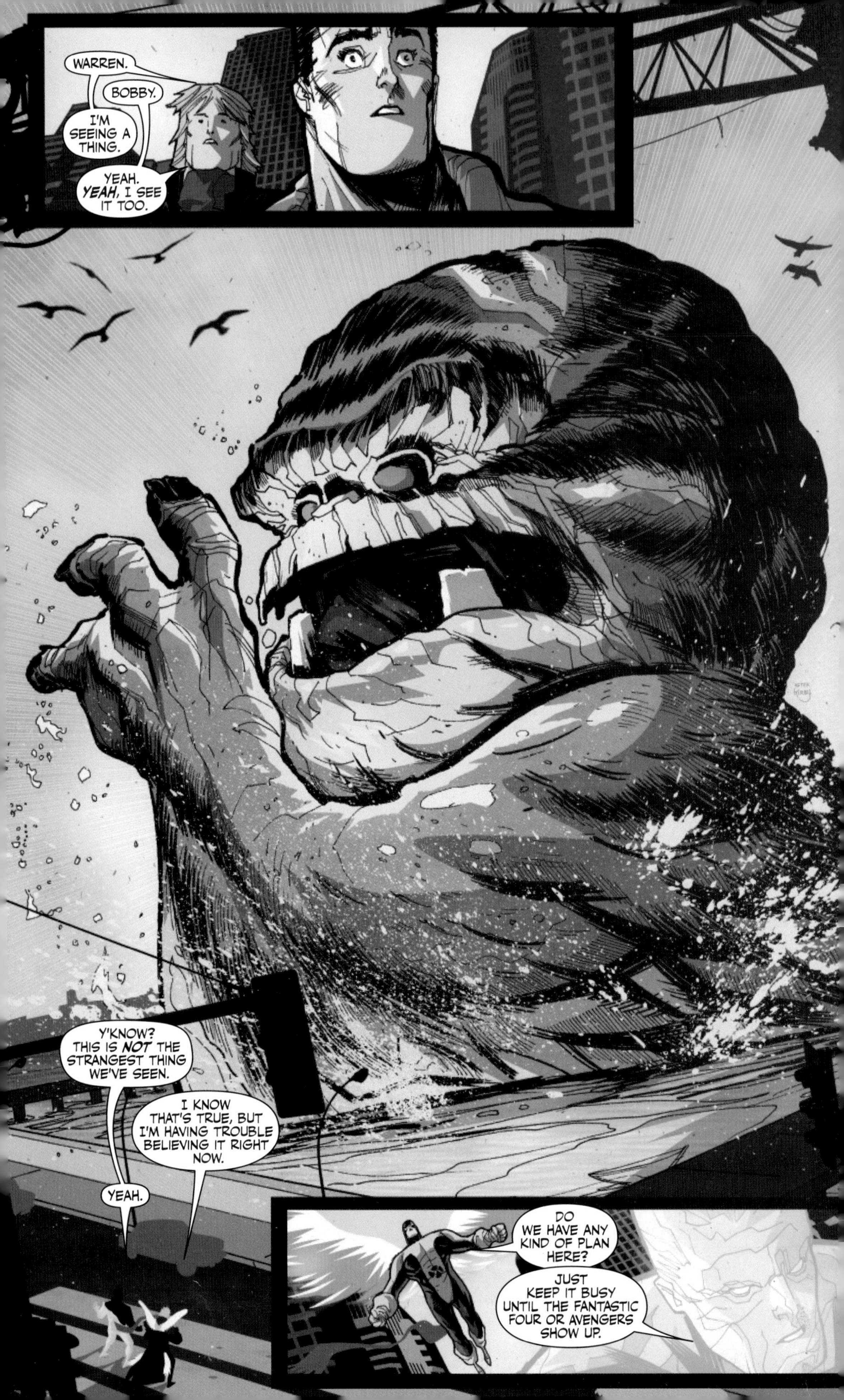

WARREN.
BOBBY.
I'M SEEING A THING.
YEAH. *YEAH*, I SEE IT TOO.
Y'KNOW? THIS IS *NOT* THE STRANGEST THING WE'VE SEEN.
I KNOW THAT'S TRUE, BUT I'M HAVING TROUBLE BELIEVING IT RIGHT NOW.
YEAH.
DO WE HAVE ANY KIND OF PLAN HERE?
JUST KEEP IT BUSY UNTIL THE FANTASTIC FOUR OR AVENGERS SHOW UP.

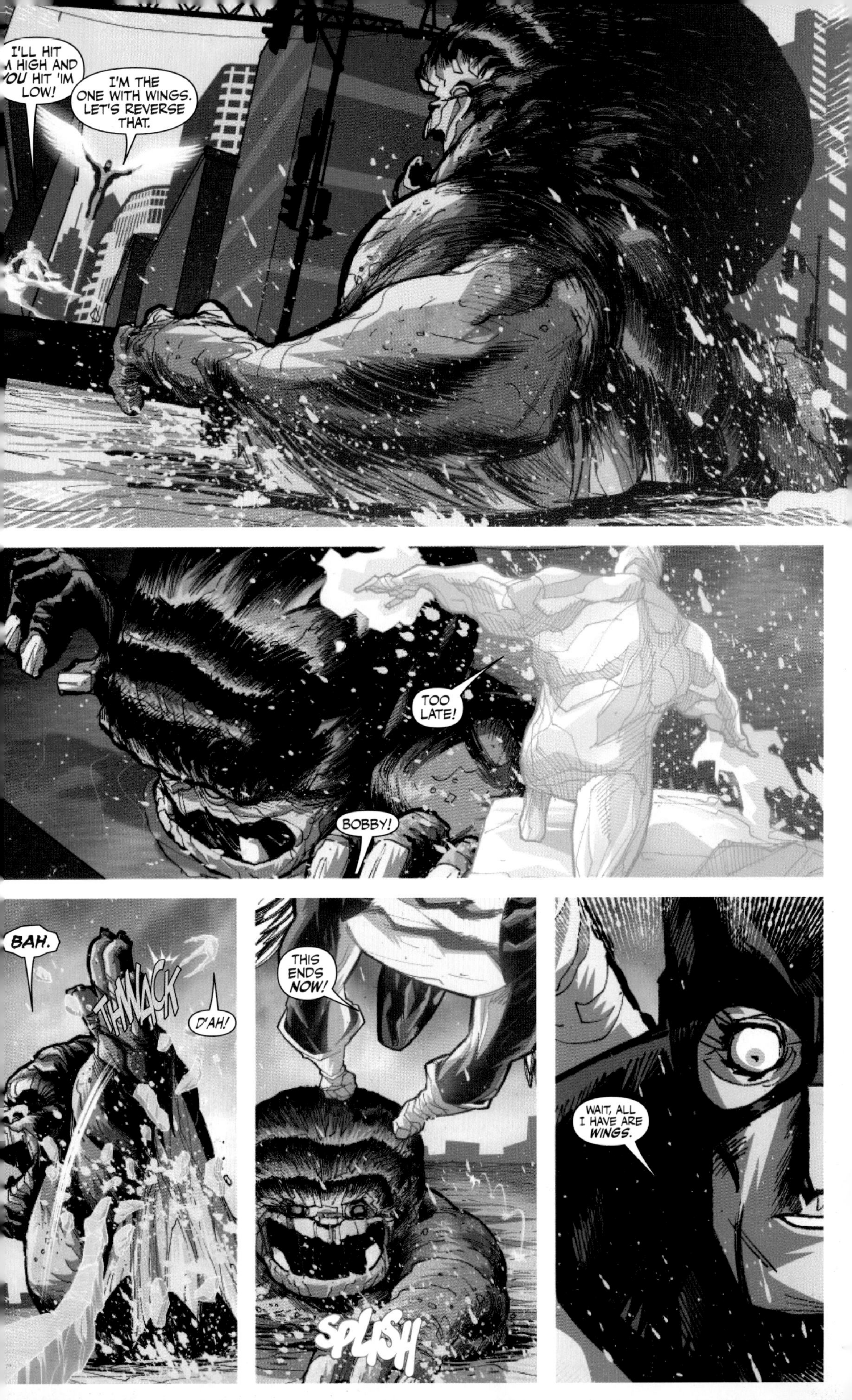
I'LL HIT 'IM HIGH AND YOU HIT 'IM LOW!
I'M THE ONE WITH WINGS. LET'S REVERSE THAT.
TOO LATE!
BOBBY!
BAH.
THWACK
D'AH!
THIS ENDS NOW!
SPLISH
WAIT, ALL I HAVE ARE WINGS.

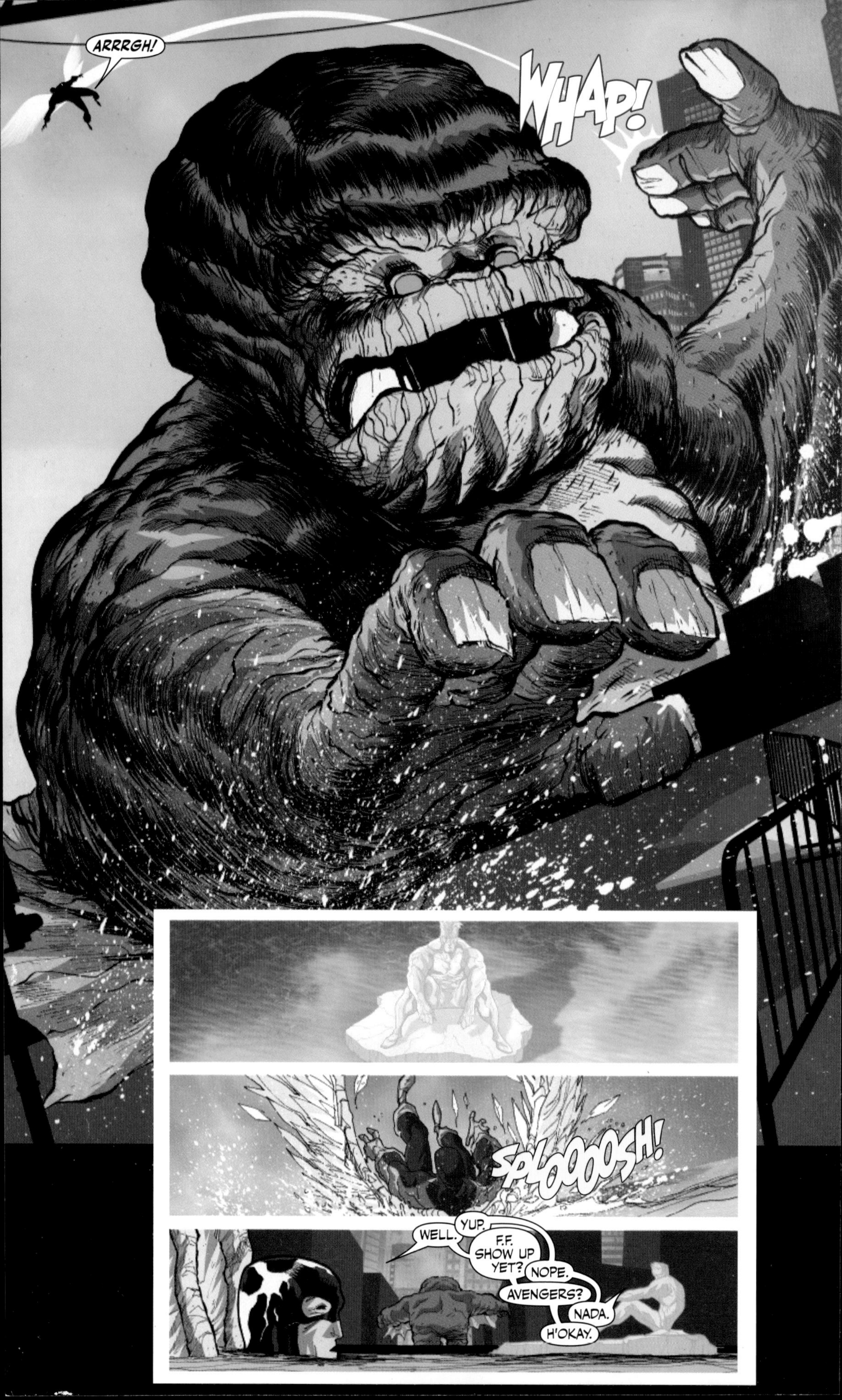

ARRRGH!
WHAP!
SPLOOOOSH!
WELL.
YUP.
F.F. SHOW UP YET?
NOPE.
AVENGERS?
NADA.
H'OKAY.

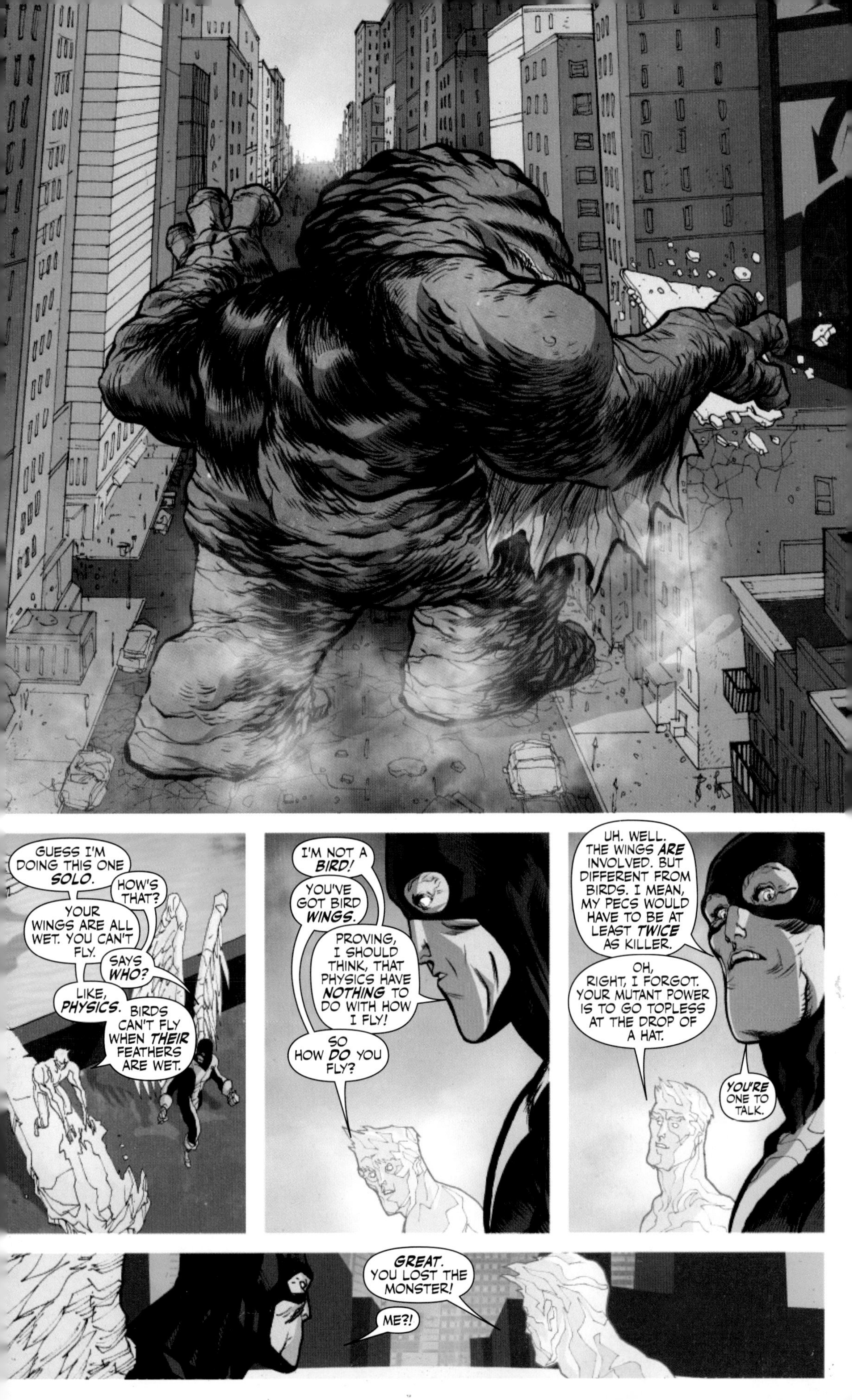
GUESS I'M DOING THIS ONE SOLO.
HOW'S THAT?
YOUR WINGS ARE ALL WET. YOU CAN'T FLY.
SAYS WHO?
LIKE, PHYSICS.
BIRDS CAN'T FLY WHEN THEIR FEATHERS ARE WET.
I'M NOT A BIRD!
YOU'VE GOT BIRD WINGS.
PROVING, I SHOULD THINK, THAT PHYSICS HAVE NOTHING TO DO WITH HOW I FLY!
SO HOW DO YOU FLY?
UH. WELL. THE WINGS ARE INVOLVED. BUT DIFFERENT FROM BIRDS. I MEAN, MY PECS WOULD HAVE TO BE AT LEAST TWICE AS KILLER.
OH, RIGHT, I FORGOT. YOUR MUTANT POWER IS TO GO TOPLESS AT THE DROP OF A HAT.
YOU'RE ONE TO TALK.
GREAT. YOU LOST THE MONSTER!
ME?!

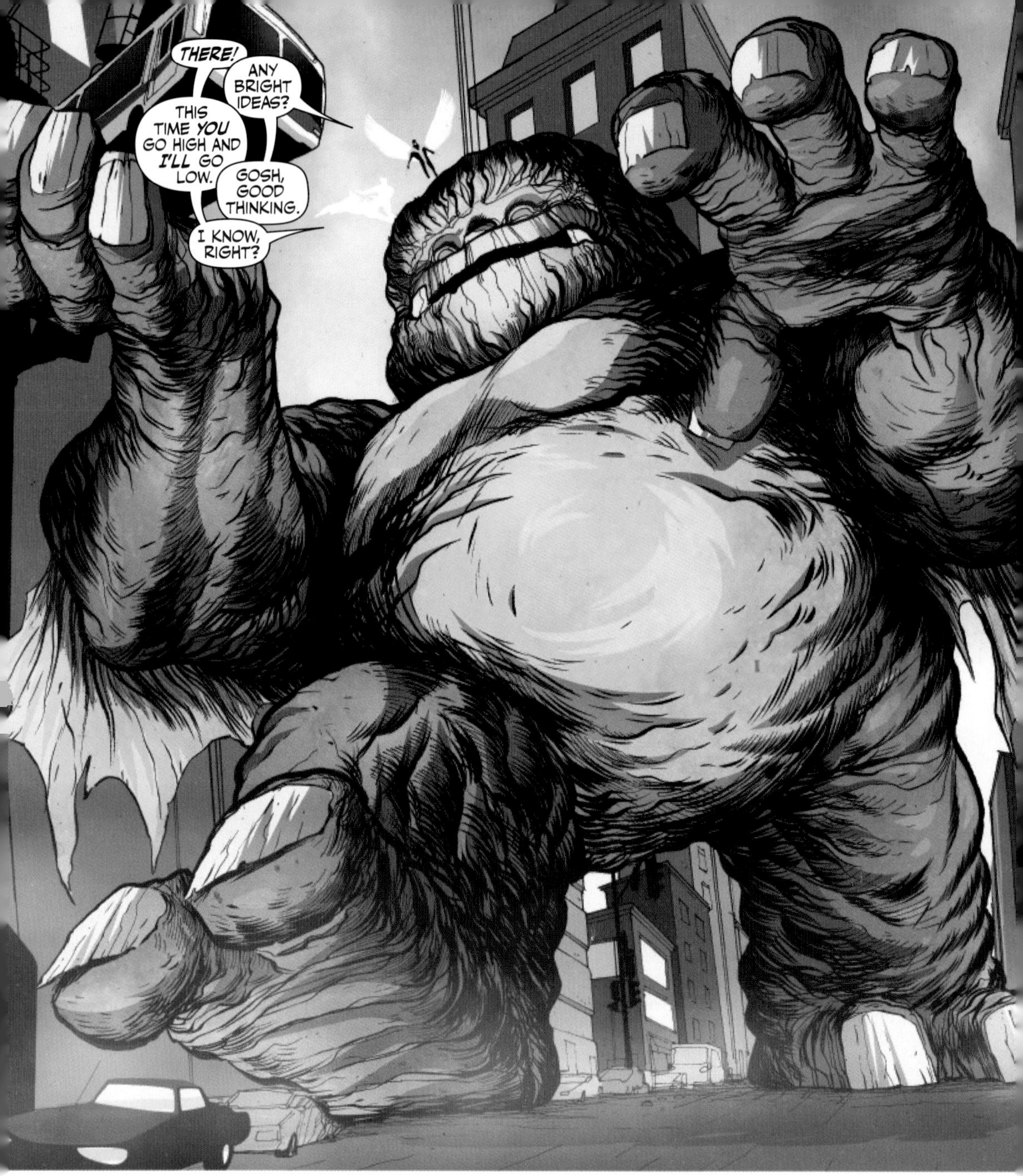
THERE!
ANY BRIGHT IDEAS?
THIS TIME YOU GO HIGH AND I'LL GO LOW.
GOSH, GOOD THINKING.
I KNOW, RIGHT?

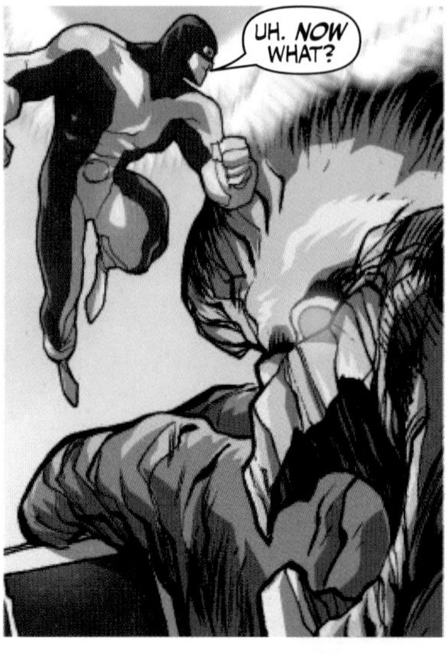
UH. NOW WHAT?

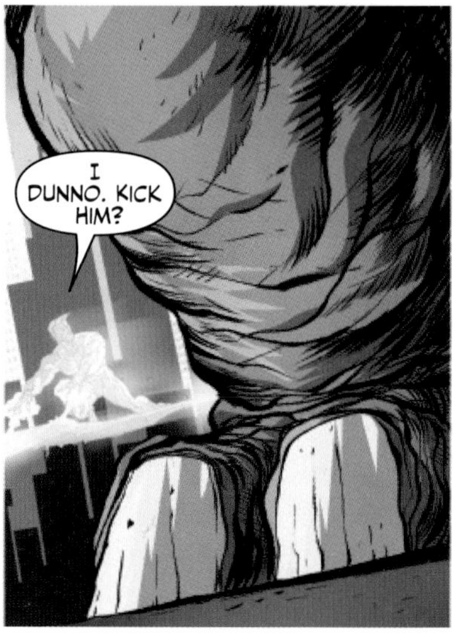
I DUNNO. KICK HIM?

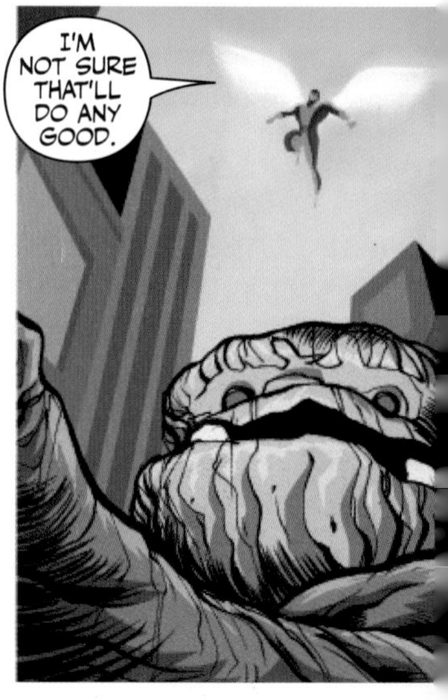
I'M NOT SURE THAT'LL DO ANY GOOD.

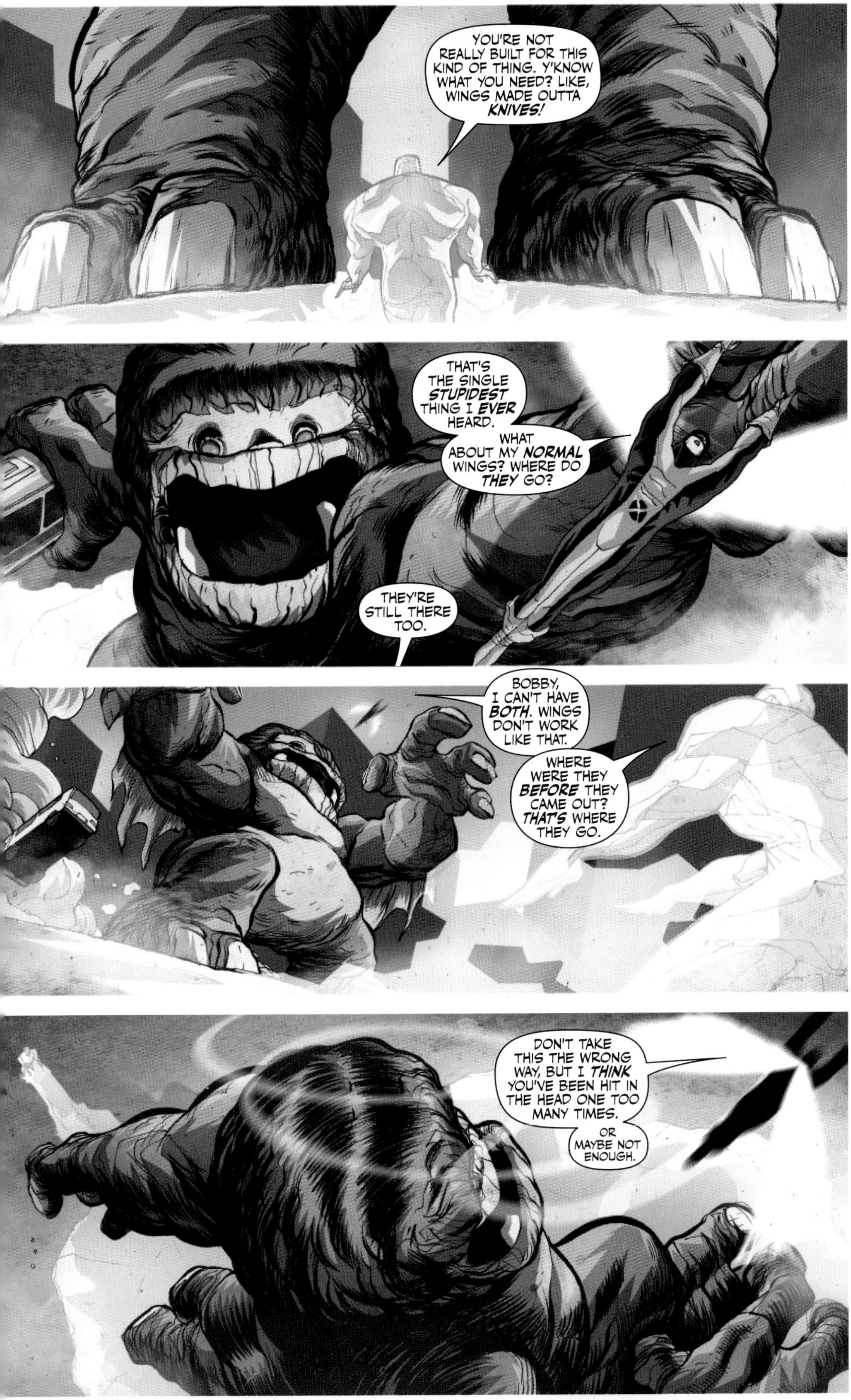
YOU'RE NOT REALLY BUILT FOR THIS KIND OF THING. Y'KNOW WHAT YOU NEED? LIKE, WINGS MADE OUTTA KNIVES!
THAT'S THE SINGLE STUPIDEST THING I EVER HEARD.
WHAT ABOUT MY NORMAL WINGS? WHERE DO THEY GO?
THEY'RE STILL THERE TOO.
BOBBY, I CAN'T HAVE BOTH. WINGS DON'T WORK LIKE THAT.
WHERE WERE THEY BEFORE THEY CAME OUT? THAT'S WHERE THEY GO.
DON'T TAKE THIS THE WRONG WAY, BUT I THINK YOU'VE BEEN HIT IN THE HEAD ONE TOO MANY TIMES.
OR MAYBE NOT ENOUGH.

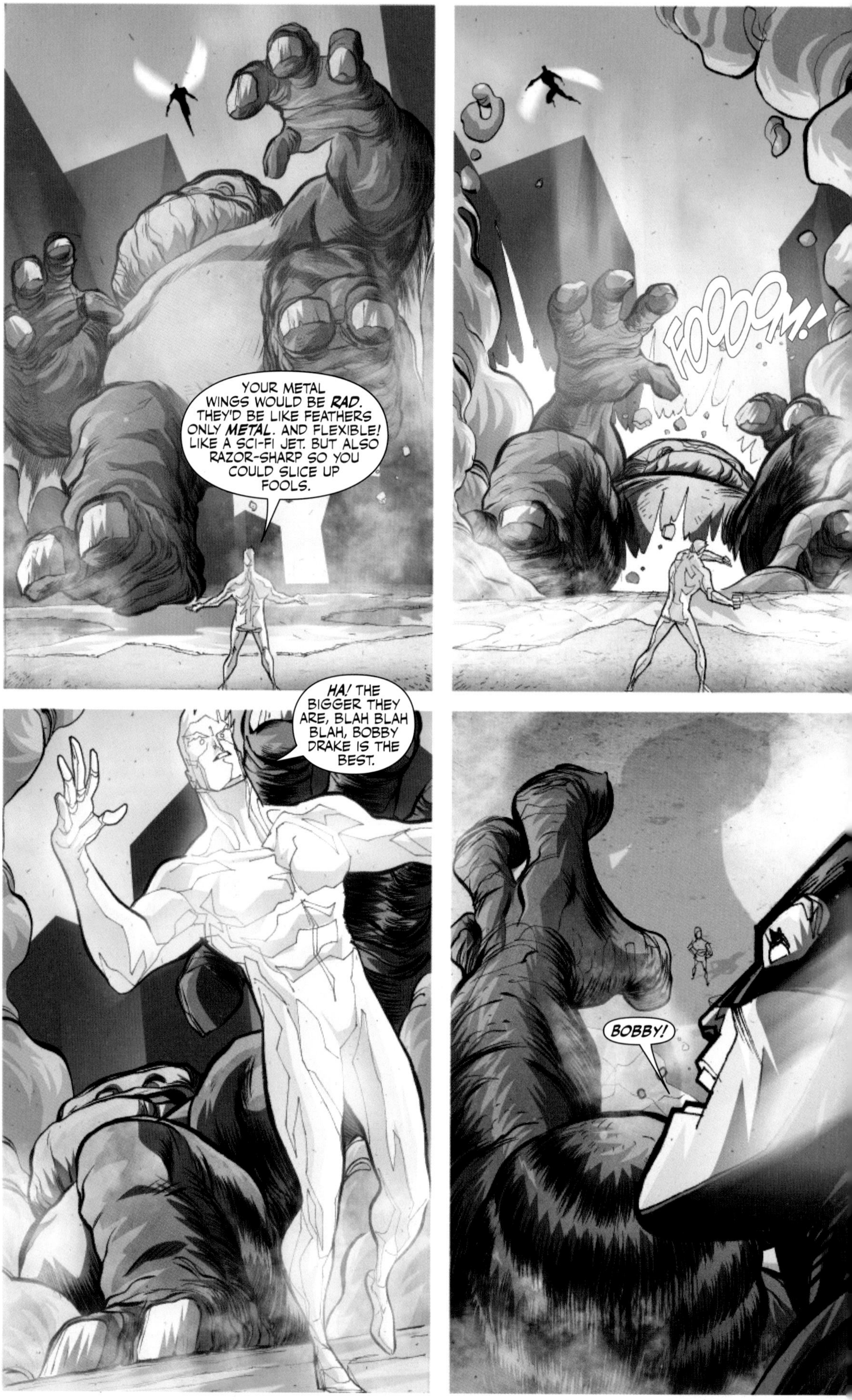
YOUR METAL WINGS WOULD BE RAD. THEY'D BE LIKE FEATHERS ONLY METAL. AND FLEXIBLE! LIKE A SCI-FI JET. BUT ALSO RAZOR-SHARP SO YOU COULD SLICE UP FOOLS.
FOOOOM!
HA! THE BIGGER THEY ARE, BLAH BLAH BLAH, BOBBY DRAKE IS THE BEST.
BOBBY!

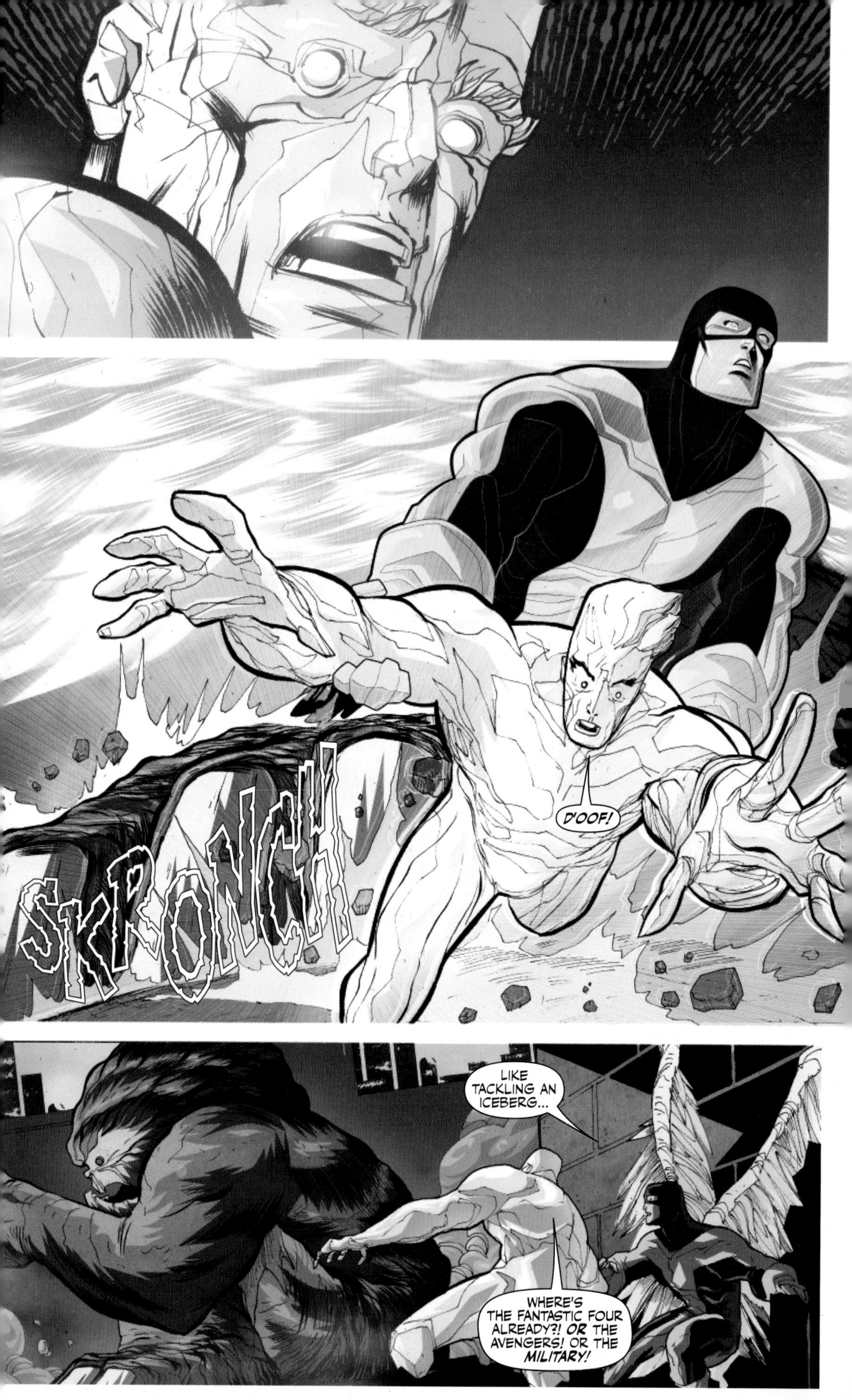
D'OOF!
SKRONCH
LIKE TACKLING AN ICEBERG...
WHERE'S THE FANTASTIC FOUR ALREADY?! OR THE AVENGERS! OR THE MILITARY!

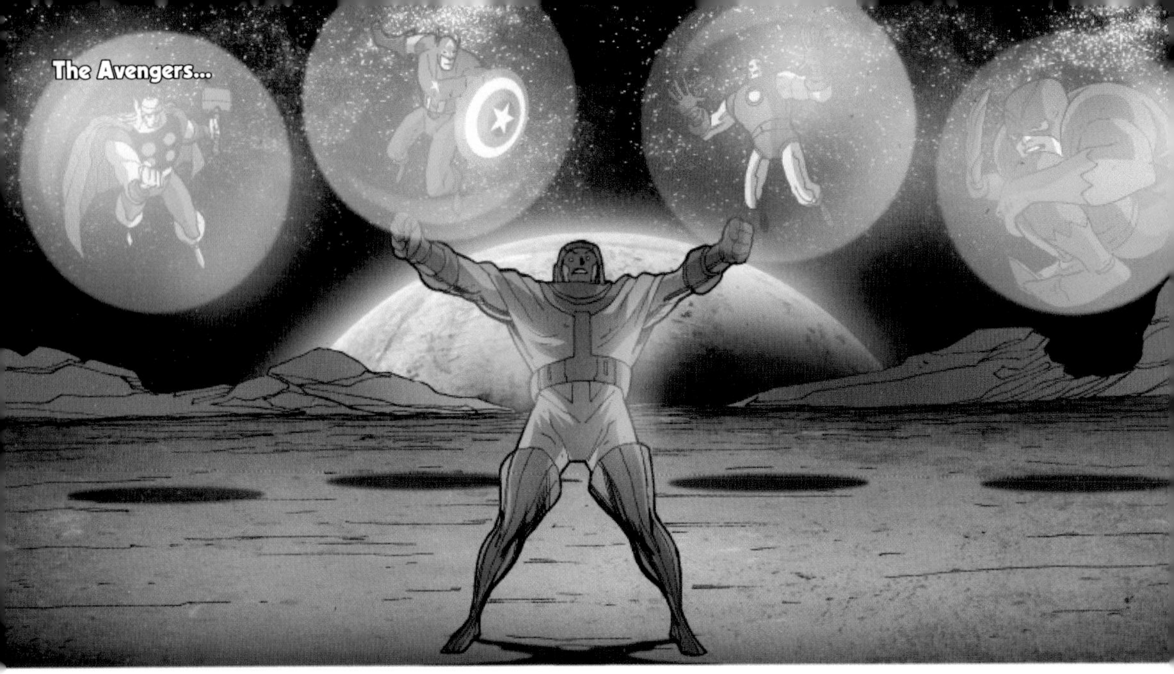
The Avengers...

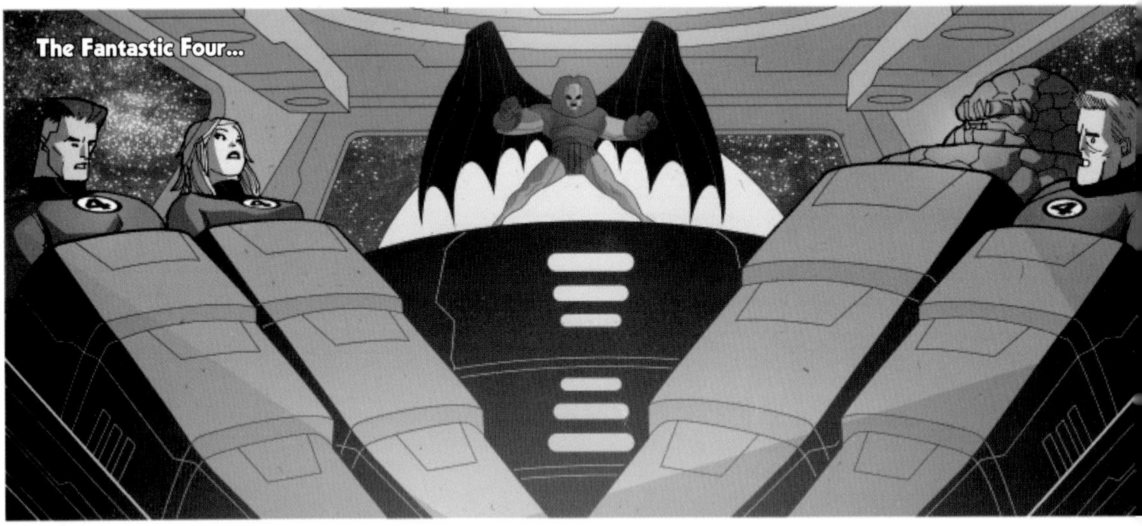
The Fantastic Four...

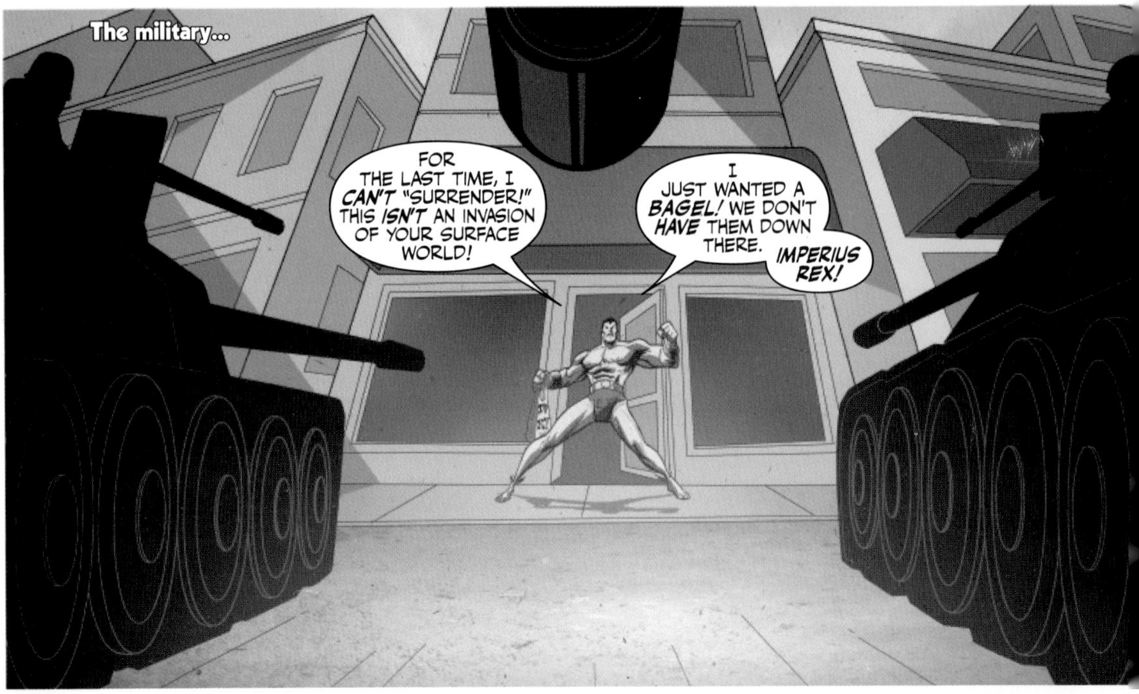
The military...
FOR THE LAST TIME, I CAN'T "SURRENDER!" THIS ISN'T AN INVASION OF YOUR SURFACE WORLD!
I JUST WANTED A BAGEL! WE DON'T HAVE THEM DOWN THERE.
IMPERIUS REX!

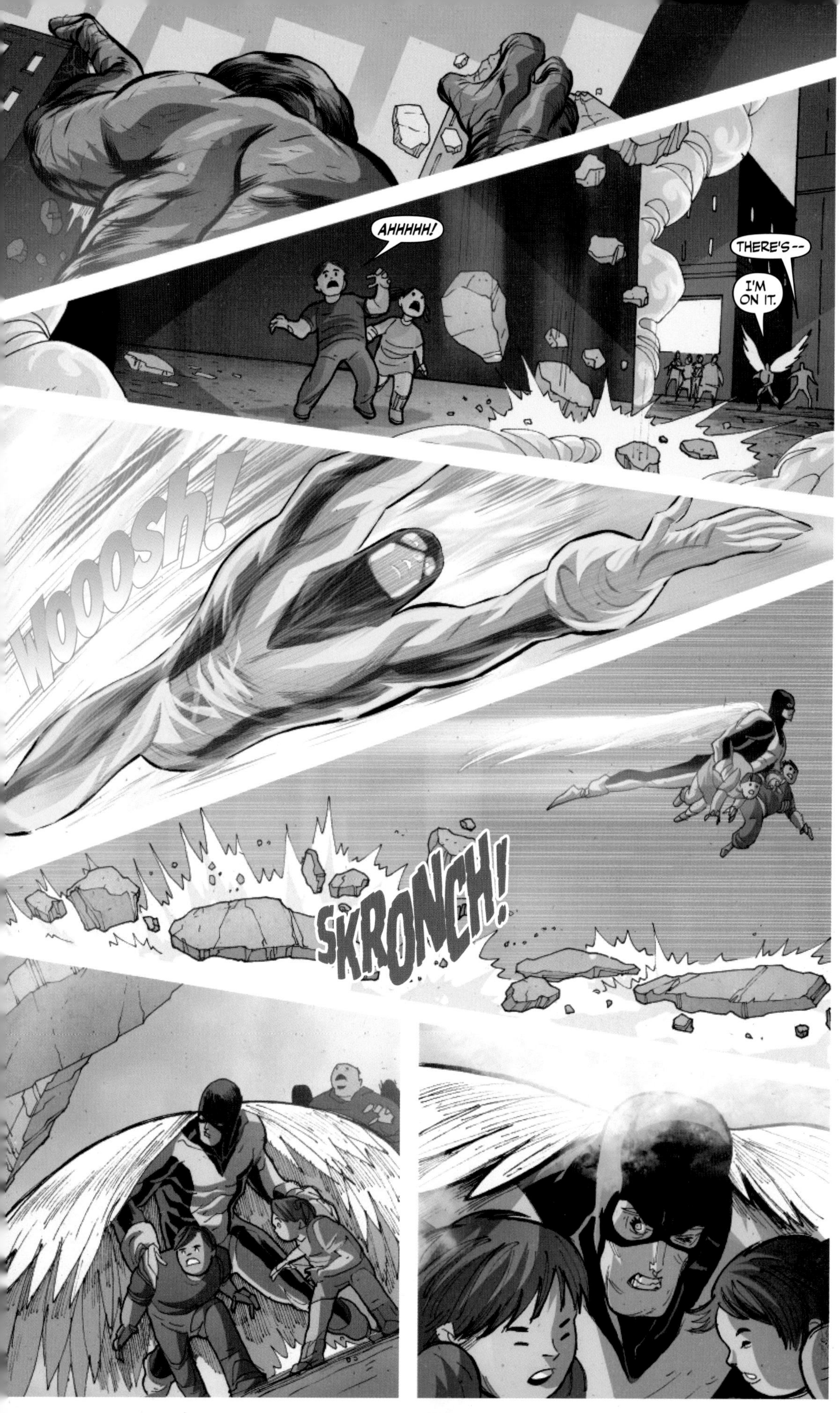
AHHHHH!
THERE'S--
I'M ON IT.
WOOOSH!
SKRONCH!

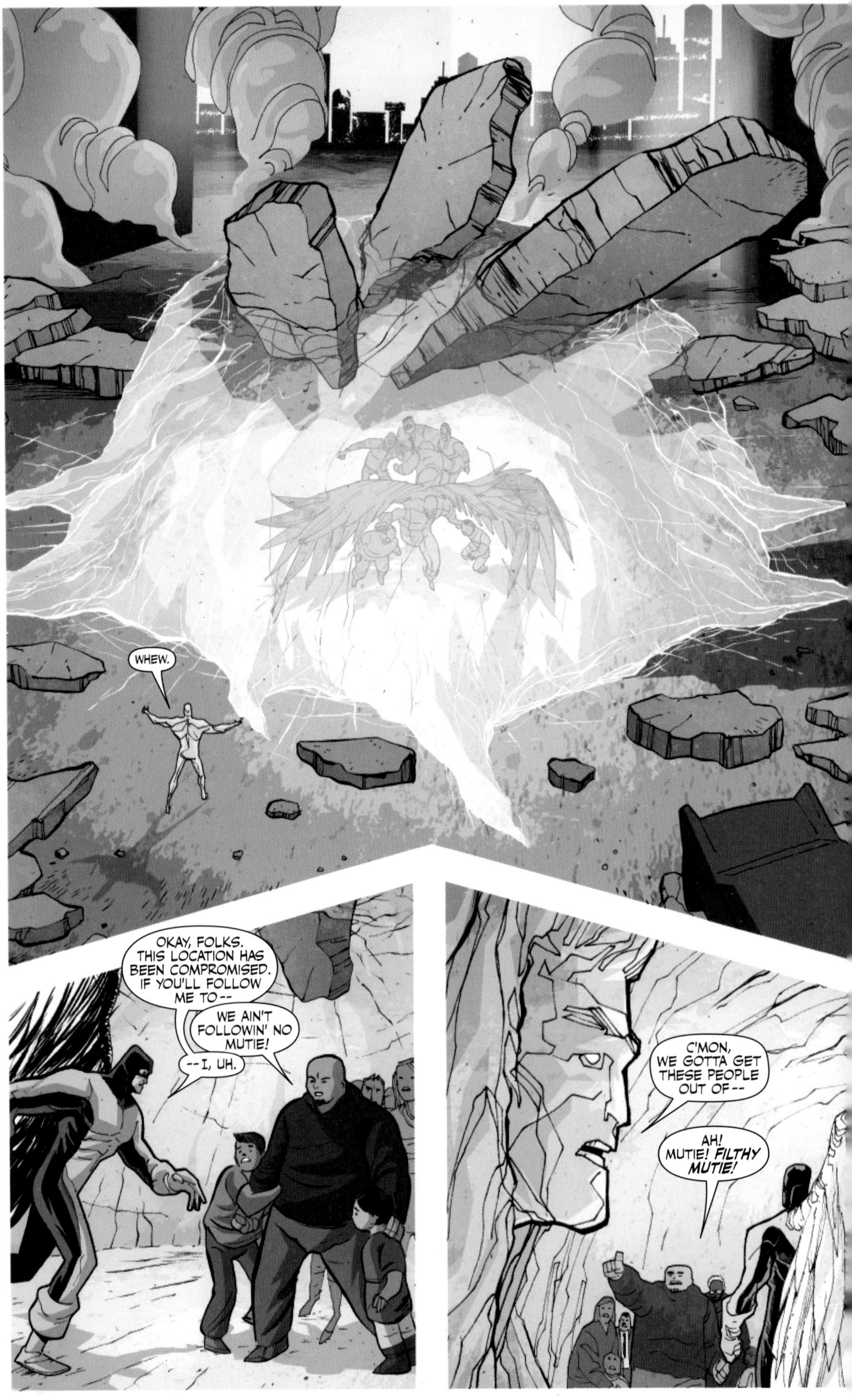
WHEW.
OKAY, FOLKS. THIS LOCATION HAS BEEN COMPROMISED. IF YOU'LL FOLLOW ME TO--
WE AIN'T FOLLOWIN' NO MUTIE!
--I, UH.
C'MON, WE GOTTA GET THESE PEOPLE OUT OF--
AH! MUTIE! *FILTHY MUTIE!*

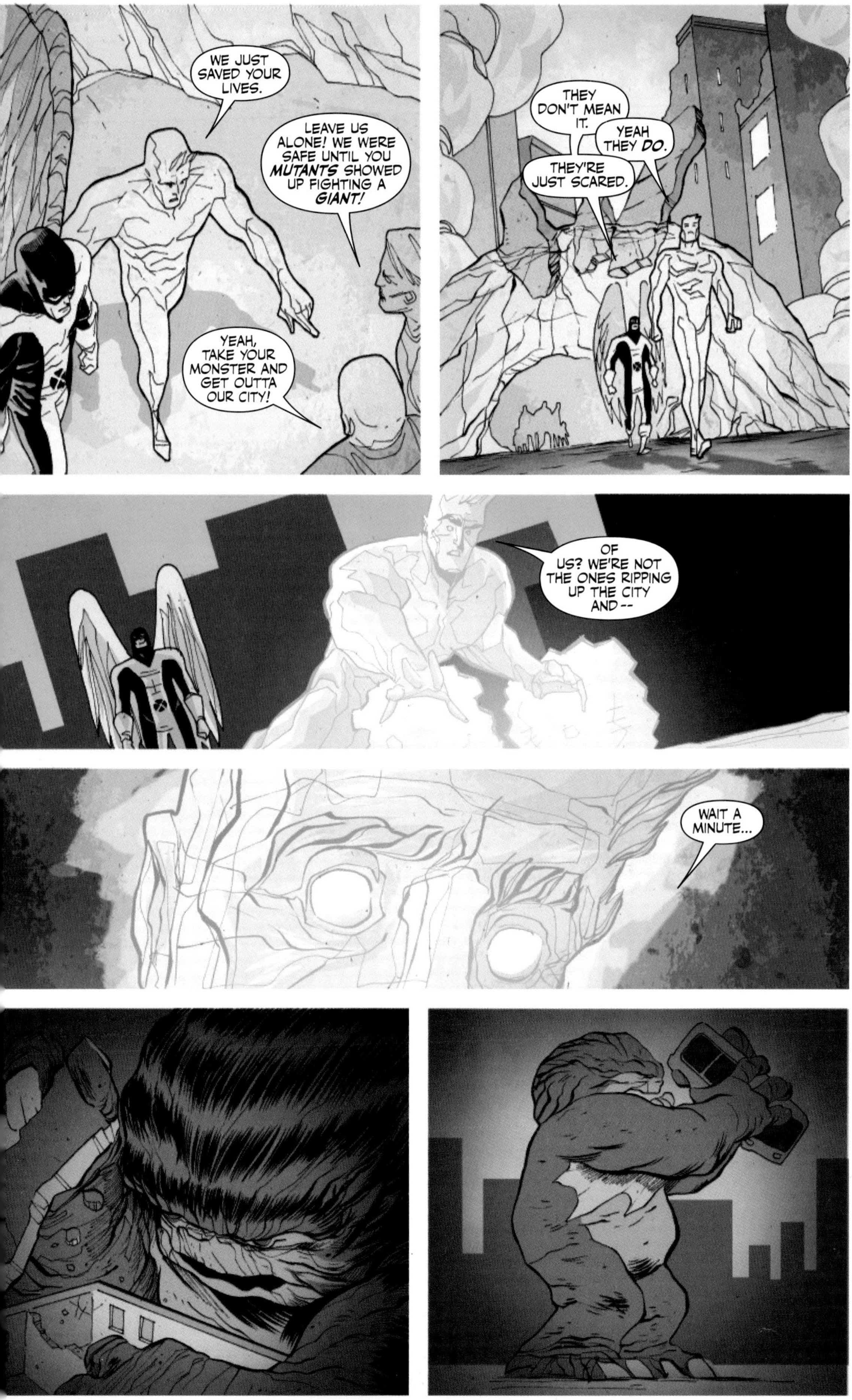

WE JUST SAVED YOUR LIVES.
LEAVE US ALONE! WE WERE SAFE UNTIL YOU MUTANTS SHOWED UP FIGHTING A GIANT!
YEAH, TAKE YOUR MONSTER AND GET OUTTA OUR CITY!
THEY DON'T MEAN IT.
THEY'RE JUST SCARED.
YEAH THEY DO.
OF US? WE'RE NOT THE ONES RIPPING UP THE CITY AND --
WAIT A MINUTE...

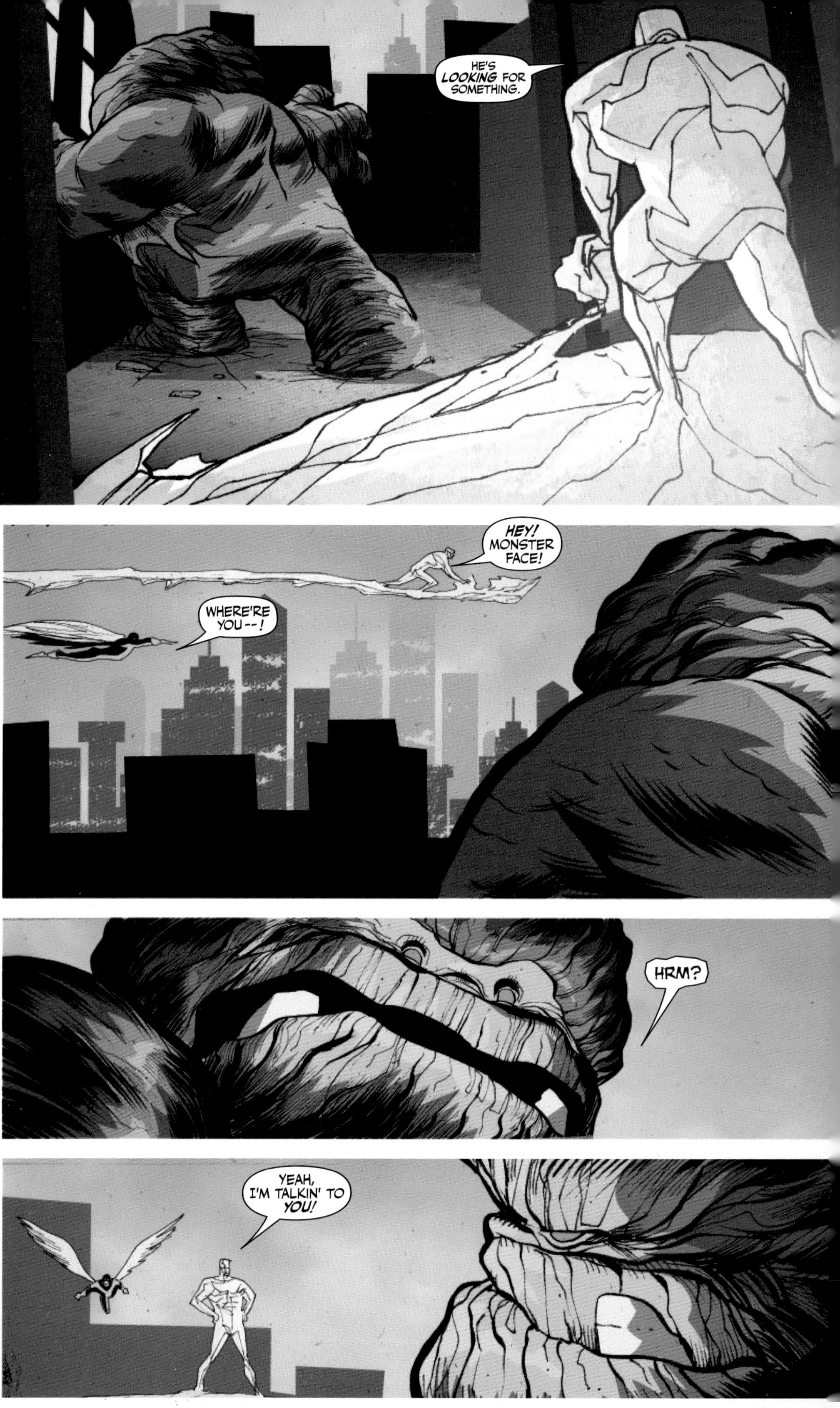
HE'S *LOOKING* FOR SOMETHING.
HEY! MONSTER FACE!
WHERE'RE YOU--!
HRM?
YEAH, I'M TALKIN' TO *YOU!*

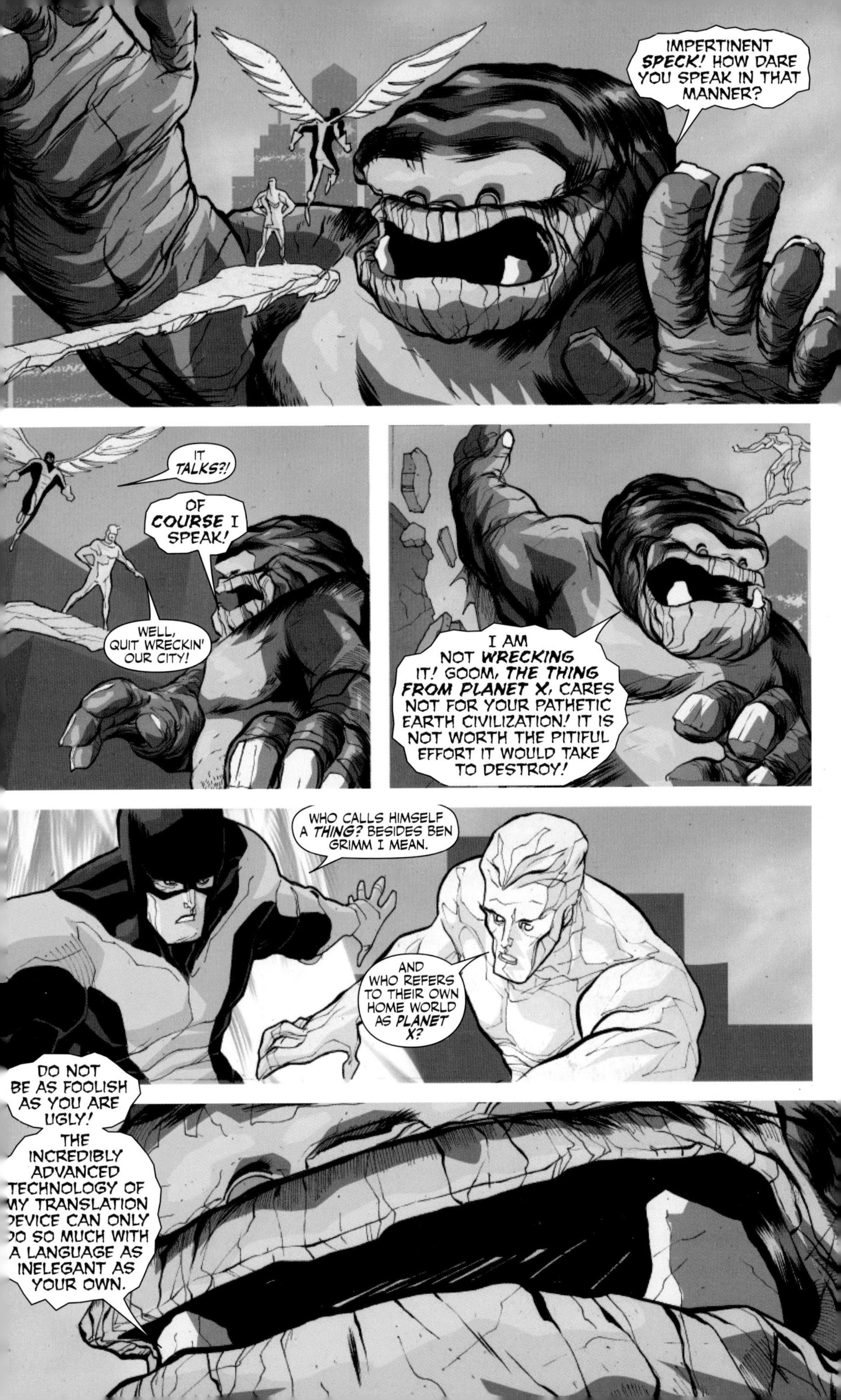

IMPERTINENT SPECK! HOW DARE YOU SPEAK IN THAT MANNER?
IT TALKS?!
OF COURSE I SPEAK!
WELL, QUIT WRECKIN' OUR CITY!
I AM NOT WRECKING IT! GOOM, THE THING FROM PLANET X, CARES NOT FOR YOUR PATHETIC EARTH CIVILIZATION! IT IS NOT WORTH THE PITIFUL EFFORT IT WOULD TAKE TO DESTROY!
WHO CALLS HIMSELF A THING? BESIDES BEN GRIMM I MEAN.
AND WHO REFERS TO THEIR OWN HOME WORLD AS PLANET X?
DO NOT BE AS FOOLISH AS YOU ARE UGLY!
THE INCREDIBLY ADVANCED TECHNOLOGY OF MY TRANSLATION DEVICE CAN ONLY DO SO MUCH WITH A LANGUAGE AS INELEGANT AS YOUR OWN.

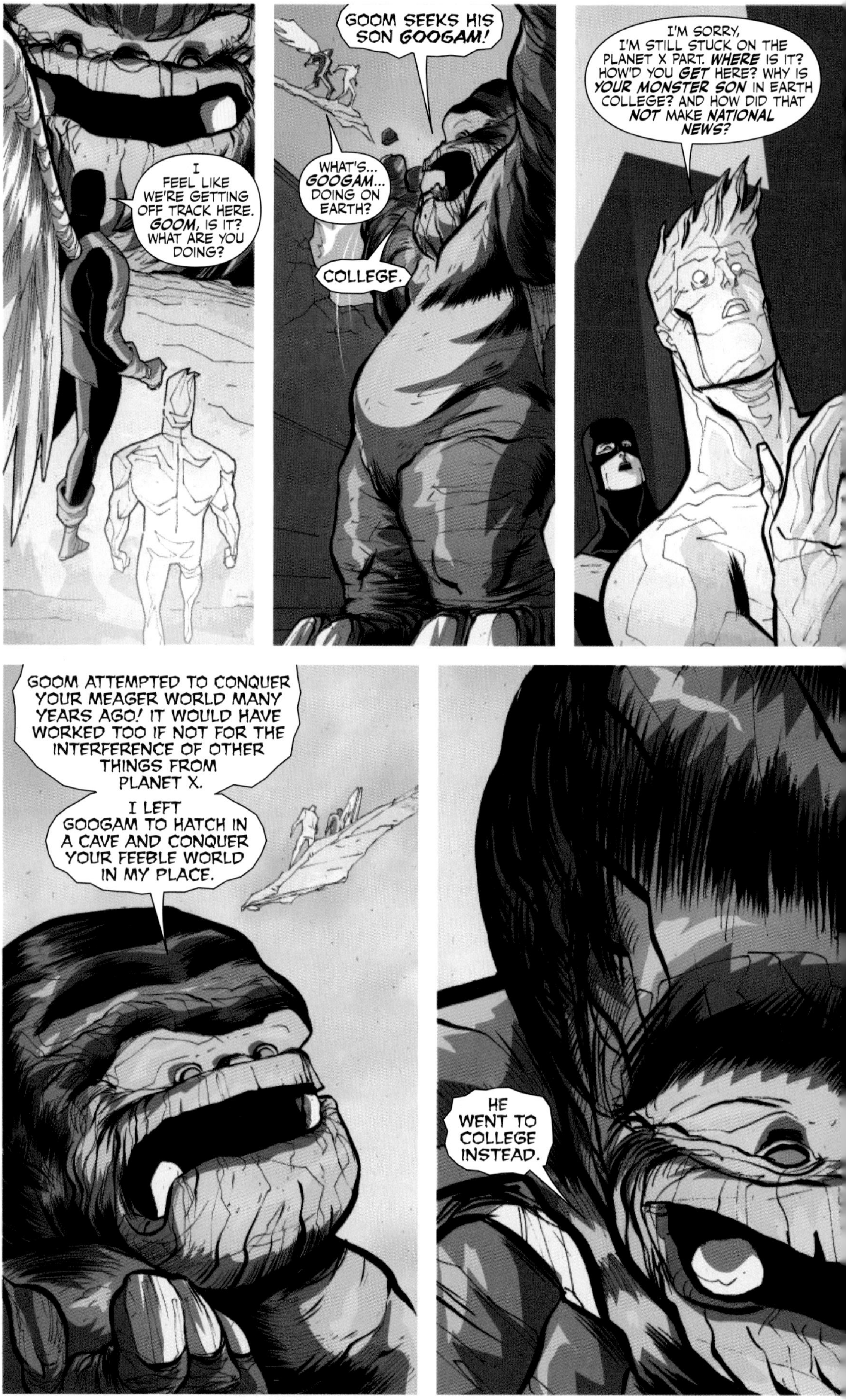
I FEEL LIKE WE'RE GETTING OFF TRACK HERE. **GOOM**, IS IT? WHAT ARE YOU DOING?
GOOM SEEKS HIS SON **GOOGAM!**
WHAT'S... **GOOGAM**... DOING ON EARTH?
COLLEGE.
I'M SORRY, I'M STILL STUCK ON THE PLANET X PART. **WHERE** IS IT? HOW'D YOU **GET** HERE? WHY IS **YOUR MONSTER SON** IN EARTH COLLEGE? AND HOW DID THAT **NOT** MAKE **NATIONAL NEWS?**
GOOM ATTEMPTED TO CONQUER YOUR MEAGER WORLD MANY YEARS AGO! IT WOULD HAVE WORKED TOO IF NOT FOR THE INTERFERENCE OF OTHER THINGS FROM PLANET X.
I LEFT GOOGAM TO HATCH IN A CAVE AND CONQUER YOUR FEEBLE WORLD IN MY PLACE.
HE WENT TO COLLEGE INSTEAD.

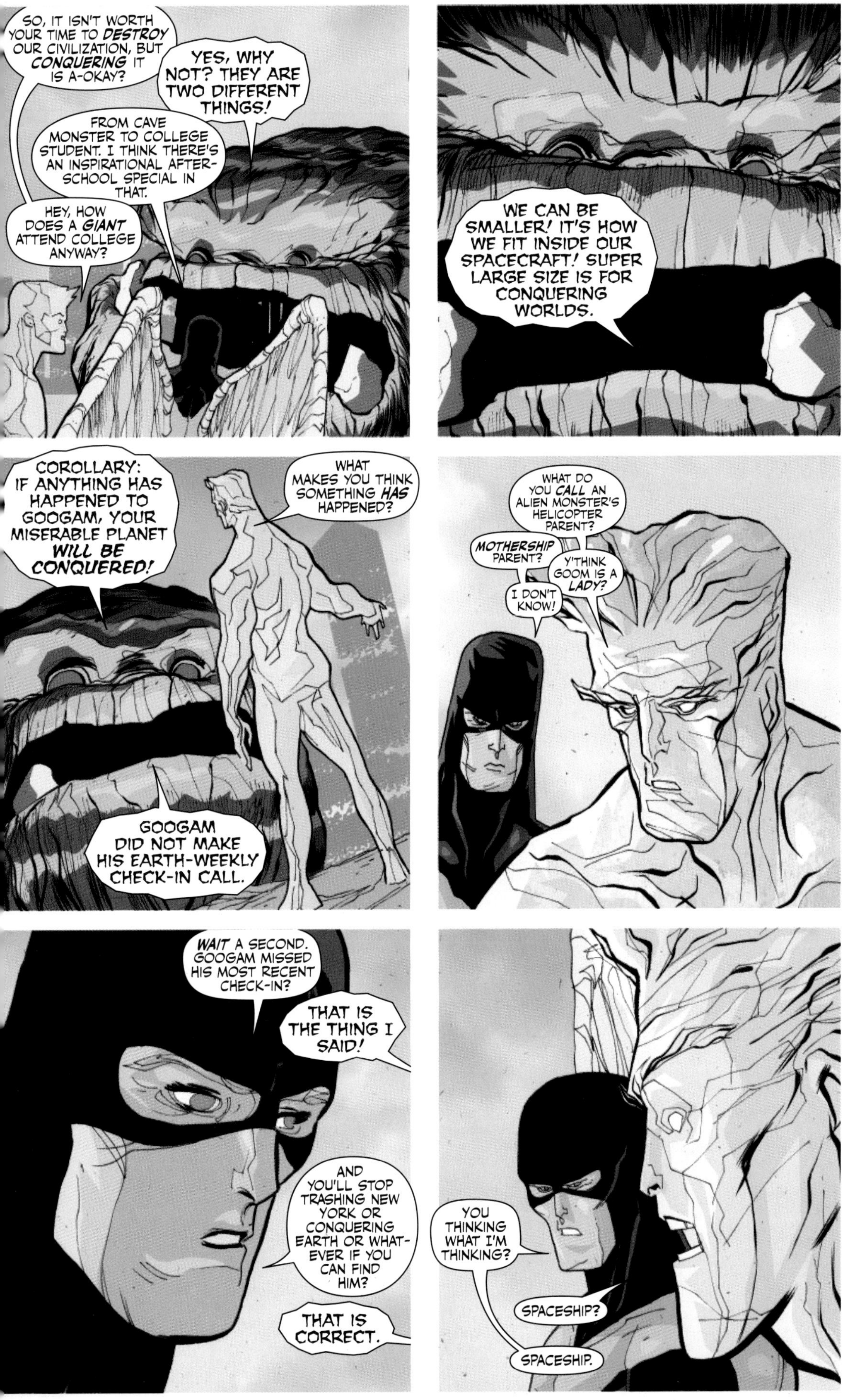
SO, IT ISN'T WORTH YOUR TIME TO DESTROY OUR CIVILIZATION, BUT CONQUERING IT IS A-OKAY?
YES, WHY NOT? THEY ARE TWO DIFFERENT THINGS!
FROM CAVE MONSTER TO COLLEGE STUDENT. I THINK THERE'S AN INSPIRATIONAL AFTER-SCHOOL SPECIAL IN THAT.
HEY, HOW DOES A GIANT ATTEND COLLEGE ANYWAY?
WE CAN BE SMALLER! IT'S HOW WE FIT INSIDE OUR SPACECRAFT! SUPER LARGE SIZE IS FOR CONQUERING WORLDS.
COROLLARY: IF ANYTHING HAS HAPPENED TO GOOGAM, YOUR MISERABLE PLANET WILL BE CONQUERED!
WHAT MAKES YOU THINK SOMETHING HAS HAPPENED?
GOOGAM DID NOT MAKE HIS EARTH-WEEKLY CHECK-IN CALL.
WHAT DO YOU CALL AN ALIEN MONSTER'S HELICOPTER PARENT?
MOTHERSHIP PARENT?
Y'THINK GOOM IS A LADY?
I DON'T KNOW!
WAIT A SECOND. GOOGAM MISSED HIS MOST RECENT CHECK-IN?
THAT IS THE THING I SAID!
AND YOU'LL STOP TRASHING NEW YORK OR CONQUERING EARTH OR WHAT-EVER IF YOU CAN FIND HIM?
THAT IS CORRECT.
YOU THINKING WHAT I'M THINKING?
SPACESHIP?
SPACESHIP.

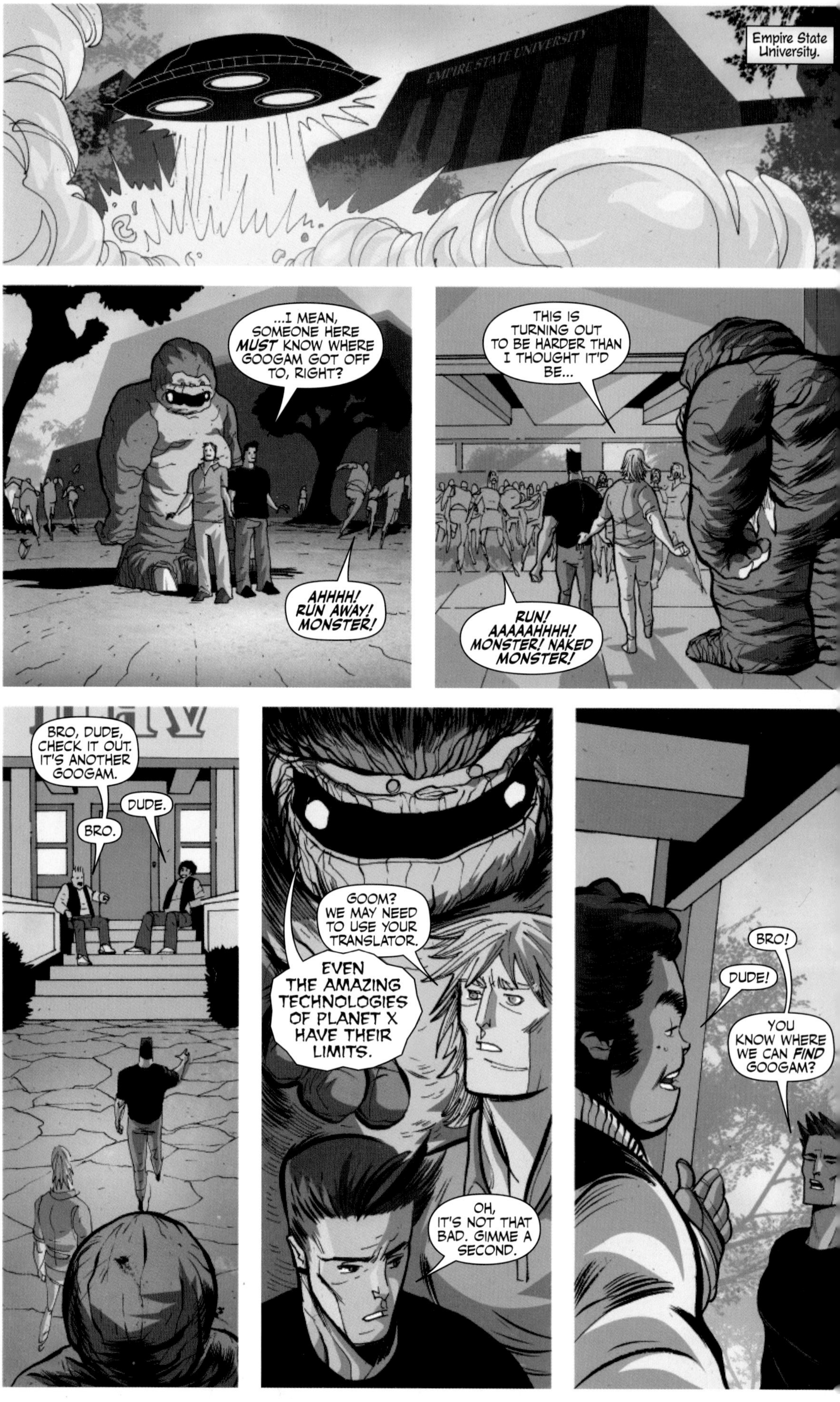
Empire State University.
EMPIRE STATE UNIVERSITY
...I MEAN, SOMEONE HERE MUST KNOW WHERE GOOGAM GOT OFF TO, RIGHT?
AHHHH! RUN AWAY! MONSTER!
THIS IS TURNING OUT TO BE HARDER THAN I THOUGHT IT'D BE...
RUN! AAAAAHHHH! MONSTER! NAKED MONSTER!
BRO, DUDE, CHECK IT OUT. IT'S ANOTHER GOOGAM.
DUDE.
BRO.
GOOM? WE MAY NEED TO USE YOUR TRANSLATOR.
EVEN THE AMAZING TECHNOLOGIES OF PLANET X HAVE THEIR LIMITS.
OH, IT'S NOT THAT BAD. GIMME A SECOND.
BRO!
DUDE!
YOU KNOW WHERE WE CAN FIND GOOGAM?

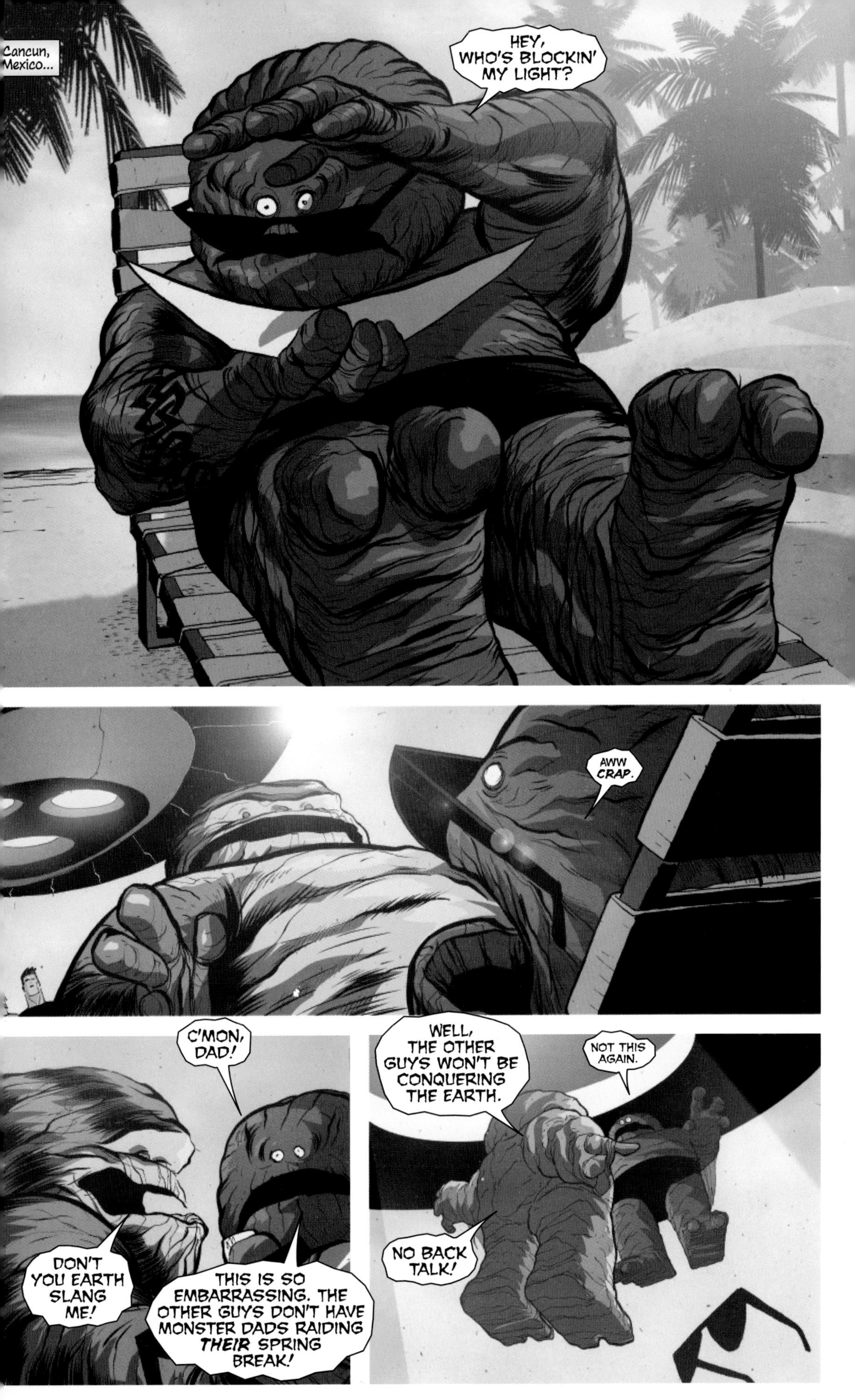
Cancun, Mexico...
HEY, WHO'S BLOCKIN' MY LIGHT?
AWW CRAP.
C'MON, DAD!
DON'T YOU EARTH SLANG ME!
THIS IS SO EMBARRASSING. THE OTHER GUYS DON'T HAVE MONSTER DADS RAIDING THEIR SPRING BREAK!
WELL, THE OTHER GUYS WON'T BE CONQUERING THE EARTH.
NOT THIS AGAIN.
NO BACK TALK!

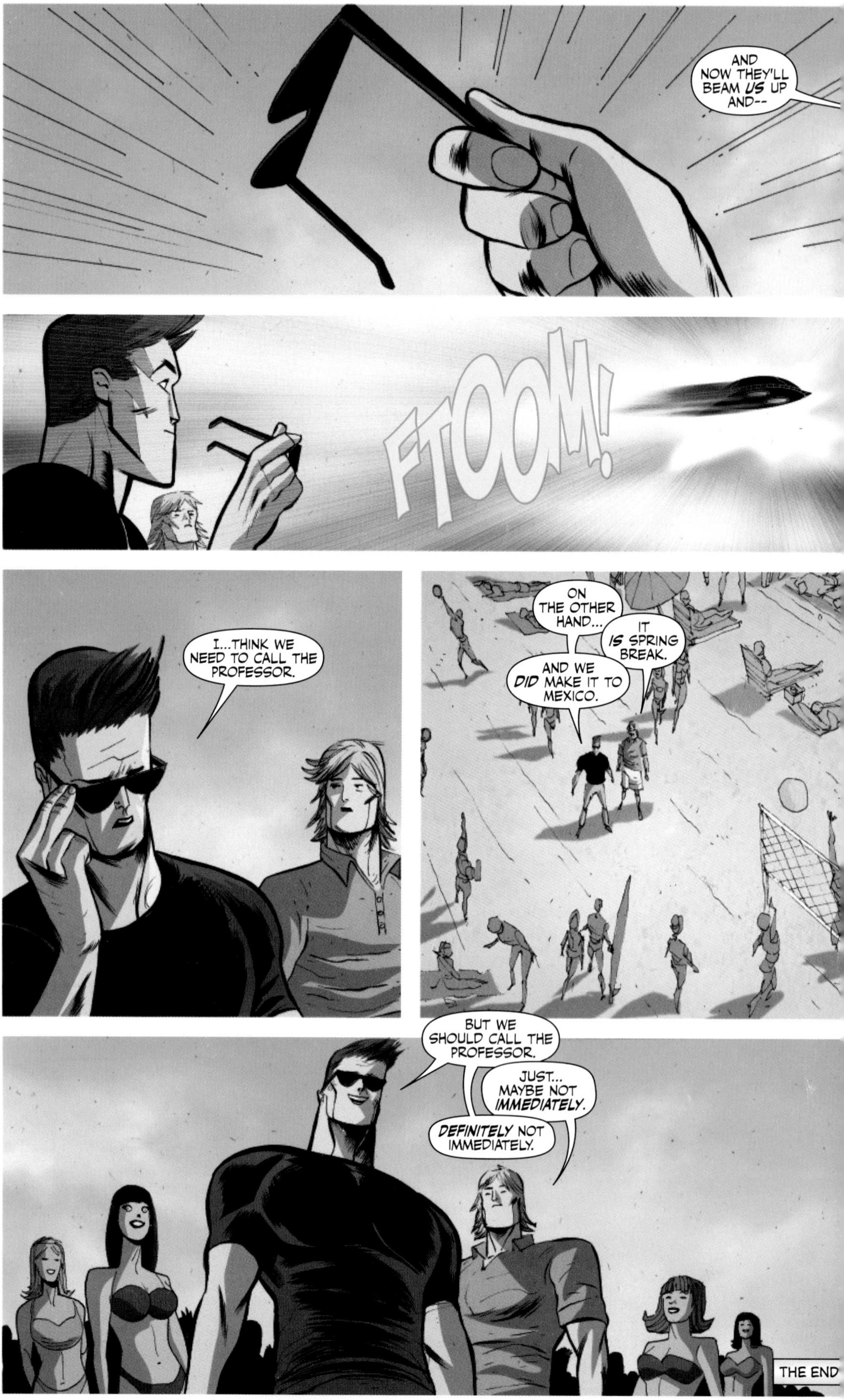
AND NOW THEY'LL BEAM *US* UP AND--
FTOOM!
I...THINK WE NEED TO CALL THE PROFESSOR.
ON THE OTHER HAND...
IT *IS* SPRING BREAK.
AND WE *DID* MAKE IT TO MEXICO.
BUT WE SHOULD CALL THE PROFESSOR.
JUST... MAYBE NOT *IMMEDIATELY*.
DEFINITELY NOT IMMEDIATELY.
THE END